About the Book

Vixie's family separated in September, when the young fox was six months old.

Throughout the fall food and shelter were plentiful, but in the winter Vixie often had to go to the farmer's barn to find food. She made friends with the farmer's cats, especially with Ginger, whose small kittens appealed to Vixie's maternal instincts. But the farmer, with his traps and poisons, was a constant threat to Vixie.

That spring Vixie and her mate, Whitepaws, had their own four cubs, and there was much to teach them before the coming fall—when they too would have to survive on their own.

Dr. Michael Fox's genuine understanding of foxes is reflected in his superb, accurate descriptions of the animals' movements and behavior. The complex interrelationships between foxes and other animals and between wildlife and the farmer are clearly shown in this engrossing, true-to-life story, illustrated with graceful, realistic drawings by Jennifer Perrott.

Vixie,

THE STORY OF
A LITTLE FOX

Vixie,

THE STORY OF
A LITTLE FOX

by Dr. Michael Fox

ILLUSTRATED BY JENNIFER PERROTT

Coward, McCann & Geoghegan, Inc.   New York

For Camilla—

my own little vixen

Contents

Vixie,

THE STORY OF

A LITTLE FOX

1
Alone

Her full name was April Acorn Vixen the
seventh because she was born in April in a den
under the old oak tree, and she was the seventh
girl fox, or vixen, to be born there.

Vixie lived in the lush, cool countryside of
eastern Pennsylvania. Although she was an American fox by birth, she had English blood in her

too. Many generations ago, some local residents who liked the English sport of fox hunting found that there was a shortage of local American foxes. They imported some red foxes from England. Fortunately, not all these foxes were chased down and killed during the fox hunts. Many of them outwitted the hunters, settled down, and eventually mated with the American foxes. This was Vixie's heritage.

But all this meant nothing to Vixie. All that mattered was that she was alone, very alone, for the first time in her life. She had woken up and crawled out of the den into the misty sunshine of a crisp fall morning. She had sniffed the air and given a musical "cu-cu-cu-coo" call to her two brothers, Long-tail and Rufus, but they had not answered.

She felt the same emptiness now that she had felt a few weeks earlier when her mother and father came back with food after a night's hunt. But they had left immediately and never returned again.

Vixie also felt a sense of freedom. The whole hillside and meadows were hers, with no rough brothers to compete with. Foxes and man are alike in that they enjoy company sometimes, but they also like to be left alone to fend for themselves and to do whatever they want.

But Vixie was only six months old. How could she possibly survive all the dangers ahead? And how could she catch enough food to keep that bottomless pit, her stomach, from grumbling every few hours?

Fortunately, her parents hadn't spoiled her with too much food, so that when they were away hunting, she and her brothers had learned to hunt for themselves. They caught beetles and grasshoppers, mice and voles, and even enjoyed blackberries and wild crab apples that the wind had blown from the trees. And when they weren't hunting, they played for hours, practicing how to defend themselves if they were attacked by another fox, or even a dog. They also learned how to stalk and ambush so that later they could catch rabbits and birds like ducks and pheasants.

It may seem cruel to human beings that animals like wolves and coyotes and foxes kill weaker animals for food. But this is part of the balance of nature, a relationship that has evolved over hundreds of thousands of years, long before man appeared on earth. The small animals that Vixie and animals like her live on produce more offspring than they can support every year, so larger animals live off the surplus. If they weren't around, the surplus animals would eat up all their own food and soon starve to death. Sometimes this does happen when the foxes don't eat enough mice and voles. Then when mice and voles become scarce, the foxes starve.

But Vixie, like all foxes, was concerned with now. She was hungry, lonely, a little afraid, but feeling so free and in control of her world. She skipped into the air and in one movement caught her tail, did a backward somersault, and landed on her front feet. As her hind feet came down a moment later, she leaped up again and then dived into the grass, rolling and squirming and rubbing her chest and chin into the moist, warm earth. Perhaps she was imagining that the grass was full of mice, or was her tail a rabbit? Quickly she sat up, ears pricked, and shaking her head and sneezing, she began to lick her paws and wipe her face, just like a cat. She wished that Rufus were there to groom and tickle her ears and eyelids, but it would be a long time before she would enjoy such foxy pleasures again.

Then she took off in that jaunty trot, as light as thistledown, on her four narrow black paws,

16

with tail trailing out gracefully behind, and her
eyes and ears alert for movement in the grass.
Suddenly, in midstride she froze, her weight shift-
ing to her hind feet. She tensed, her ears telling
her that there was something in the long grass.
But she could see nothing. With a graceful slow-
motion leap she landed with her outstretched
forepaws stabbing into the grass. Vixie felt some-

thing move, and with a dive and a snap she had her field mouse. She would not go hungry.

That early lonely morning she had a good breakfast. She spent the rest of the day dozing in a small scoop of earth under a hawthorn hedge that faced the relaxing milky autumn sun. By dusk she was ready to hunt again. But that night, the first of many long nights that she would face alone until the next spring, would be one night Vixie would never forget.

2
The Night Trap

Vixie moved silently into the gathering darkness, stealthily crossing an open meadow on the lookout for dinner. Her feet made tiny shadows where they brushed the silver dew from the grass. It was a crisp moonlit night, and the moist air held the smells of countless living things. Vixie was able to pick out the faint smell of a rabbit that grew stronger as she approached a clump of oak and willow trees on the far side of the meadow.

Something whisked silently over Vixie, and her fur was momentarily ruffled by the rush of air that hit her as she flattened out instinctively. It was Barnie, the young screech owl, having fun teasing Vixie with his incredible speed and silence. Like a shadow he swooped silently upon mice and voles. At night he was certainly king of the air. Although he was a screech owl, he made his home in the farmer's barn. His cousins, the barn owls proper, lived in the farmer's old dovecote, which hadn't housed doves for at least fifty years. The farmer himself liked to have Barnie and his owl cousins around because he knew that they kept the number of mice and rats down. There were too many for the farm cats to cope with. The mice and rats ate the grain and feed that he kept for the cows and pigs. But he had no respect for foxes. In every spare moment he would think of ways to get rid of them.

Vixie had been swooped upon and teased by Barnie before, and although she knew he meant no harm, she was careful. Young foxes are often caught by larger birds of prey, and in the higher hills above the valley where Vixie lived, there was a golden eagle who had feasted on many a baby fox. Vixie gave a gruff bark into the night, acknowledging Barnie's presence. Moments later, from a tree on the other side of the meadow, he gave his raucous hoot-scream, proclaiming his presence to the night.

Vixie continued toward the clump of trees from where Barnie had called. The smell of rabbit was growing stronger as she got closer. The nearer she got to the trees, the more uneasy she felt. Barnie normally hooted and screamed more than once. Why was he silent? Suddenly she heard a high-pitched scream from somewhere under the trees, and she remembered that it was like the sound a rabbit made when it had just been caught. Perhaps it was a rabbit in a poacher's snare—an easy meal for a fox—and she began to run toward the sound. But she was still uneasy about Barnie's silence, so she changed her course and approached the clump of trees from one side. The sound was like a magnet, drawing her closer and closer.

Suddenly a flashlight came on, cutting the night with its powerful beam. It swept over the grass until it picked her out. Vixie froze, paralyzed by the strong light. Her mind spun, confused,

alarmed and afraid. But Barnie's silence had alerted her, and she was prepared for the unexpected. Quickly she twisted over and dived into the cone of darkness outside the flashlight's beam. At the same instant the night exploded around

22

her, and she felt hot needles piercing her shoulder. Before she felt the pain, she was behind the trees, running along the hedgerow that would take her safely home to the den under the old oak tree.

As she made her way home, pausing now and again to lick her shoulder, she remembered that just before the blinding light came on, she had smelled man. It was the farmer, who had taken up a hiding place under the trees.

He had craftily put a live rabbit in a cage to serve as bait, and he imitated the scream of a hurt rabbit by making a sucking-squeaking noise with a moist palm against his mouth. With his flashlight and shotgun, he was all set to get a fox that night. Vixie had escaped, and he knew that he could never use the same trick again to lure that fox within shooting range. He had other tricks up his sleeve, though, and he would soon be pitting himself against the intelligence and keen instincts of Vixie.

By the time Vixie got close to her den, she was limping quite badly. Fortunately, only a few pieces of shot had hit her. She was young and healthy, and she would heal fast. As she got near the den, some instinctive sixth sense told her to be cautious. She sniffed the air and smelled the faint odor of man, but it was stale. As she edged slowly forward, she saw a pile of leaves and twigs at the entrance to the den. The smell of man was much stronger there. She took off at once and spent the night in a hollow under a fallen elm tree. Had she gone into the den, she would have set off a trap, which would have caught one of her feet and held her captive until the farmer came and got her. It was a long night for Vixie, and she had learned many things.

Early the next morning, when the farmer came to check the trap, he found one of his cats, a big tiger-striped male called Ginger. The cat had been out hunting for mice and got caught in the trap. Ginger was the farmer's wife's favorite cat, and when the farmer brought him home to be bandaged up, his wife was furious. She called the farmer a "big white hunter chasing innocent little foxes" and had no sympathy when he showed her all the scratches that Ginger had inflicted while he was being freed from the trap.

Later in the day Vixie cautiously checked out the old den, and her nose told her the full story. The farmer had even forgotten to pick up the trap after he had released Ginger because he was having such a hard time handling the hurt and indignant cat.

Since the trap had not been reset, it was safe, but Vixie didn't know this. She sniffed it cautiously, nosed some leaves over it, and then pushed it with her good leg. She was curious, and in true fox style, she left her "mark" on it. Naturalists call fox droppings "scats," and foxes will especially mark new things in their home range with their own droppings. Perhaps this gives them a familiar smell and makes the fox feel more comfortable.

When the farmer came back for the trap later that day, he had a very different reaction to Vixie's "mark." He thought she was "laughing" at him and showing contempt by messing on the trap.

This farmer owned the land on which Vixie lived and roamed. He knew little about the habits of wildlife or the benefits they could give him. He was sullen and unhappy, and like many people who resent their circumstances and take it out on others, he had a problem. The fact was that he hated being a farmer. He felt pushed into it. His father and generations before had owned and farmed this land. When the farmer had returned from college as a young man, he had felt it his duty to go into farming. Although he took on the responsibility, he took his dissatisfaction out on everyone and everything around him. He bullied his dogs, shouted at his wife, and beat his cattle unnecessarily when he herded them in for milking. And unfortunately, Vixie was one of the wild creatures who also bore the brunt of his unhappiness.

3

Winter Alone

Poking around under a wild apple tree for windfalls late one autumn evening, Vixie jumped to one side in surprise when an apple fell right beside her. She looked up and saw what at first glance seemed to be one of the farm cats, but it was clasping a branch in its forelimbs in a most peculiar way and was not holding on like a cat

with sharp claws. It also had a bushier tail than a cat and a dark stripe that ran the full length of it. From this stripe came a strong musky smell that Vixie had never encountered before. It was a distant cousin, the gray fox, the most skillful tree climber of all the fox-dog family.

Gray looked down at Vixie and gave a low growl—the tree was hers! Gray foxes are notoriously possessive. When Gray arched his back like a cat—a threat signal that Vixie recognized, but which was much more exaggerated than in a red fox—Vixie responded with a challenging click-bark. She surely had as much right to the crab apples as the gray fox. Gray arched his back even more and nearly lost his hold on the branch. He slipped and sent a shower of little apples all over Vixie. She tucked in and ate her fill, content to let things be. The tree was the gray fox's domain, and why bother going up trees when there was so much on the ground?

Seeing that Vixie was ignoring him and was fully occupied with the apples, Gray crawled down the tree silent as a shadow and cautiously sniffed the little black scent gland on Vixie's tail. Feeling him touch her in the half darkness, the startled Vixie jumped around and faced up to him, giving a wide-mouth threat gape and pushing out at him with her forelimbs at the same time. Gray twisted sideways and then, as though on invisible springs, leaped high in the air, hit the side of the tree with all four legs, and bounced to the ground. He repeated this ricocheting display four or five times and landed right in front of Vixie, stared at her, and then vanished into the darkness.

Perhaps Vixie was supposed to have done the same as he in some kind of game, which she could neither do nor fully understand. Her first encounter with this distant cousin left her puzzled and curious. Were there more of them, and were they really foxes, since they were so catlike? She would never forget his strong musky odor.

Actually most of the gray foxes that used to live in the region had moved out since the population had suffered seriously from trapping and poisoned baits. Gray foxes are less wary than red foxes, and their insatiable curiosity often gets them into trouble. They survive better in wild countryside and woodlands where there are few people to bother them. Gray was a young male who had wandered temporarily into Vixie's range from a nearby forest preserve.

Most of the gray fox population had been forced

out long ago. Another even more distant cousin of Vixie's, the wolf, had been totally destroyed in that area by earlier human settlers. Another big carnivore, or flesh-eating predator, the mountain lion, or puma, had also been eradicated years before. South of the state, coyotes were moving in, taking over the space or niche once occupied by these larger predators. Fortunately, Vixie did not have to compete with them or with the gray foxes for food. Her only rivals were local domestic cats and dogs and the occasional weasel that would pursue rabbits into their burrows with lightning speed and kill them with a single bite.

The autumn days became shorter, the nights longer, and food harder and harder to find as the tight fist of winter closed in. A heavy hoarfrost covered the meadow and rarely melted away before noon. All the juicy insects of the fall were gone, and the berries and fruits that gave each meal a banquetlike finish had been cleaned up by Vixie and her neighbors—sparrows, finches, voles and field mice. The crows and dogs and cats from surrounding farms competed with her for any other carrion, or dead food, that she might find. The fields were being picked clean by the hungry animals, and each day Vixie scoured the hedgerows for food. Occasionally she found a mouse in a plowed furrow and leaped and grabbed it before it found a safe burrow to escape down. The hard, frozen earth no longer cut her pads, for they were now hard and tough, and she had grown a thick winter coat. She used her tail as a ruff, curling it around her and under her paws when she went to sleep, usually with her nose tucked in, too. This way she was well insulated from the cold and was very comfortable sleeping out in the open, using a rock or hedge as a wind-break.

Many of the summer residents of the meadows and surrounding hillsides had left, migrating south to warmer places. Other animals like squirrels and dormice avoided the winter by sleeping or hibernating. On very warm days, some would wake up briefly and snack on a store of seeds and nuts. Vixie found a number of squirrels' winter stores and would tuck in when she was very hungry.

The first snow for Vixie came as a great surprise. She woke up one morning to find her world all white. A gentle breeze had blown snowflakes all over her thick fur. She looked just like an arctic fox but not for long. With a quick shake

she shed the snow. Her coat not only kept her warm but also was a good water repellent, because of its dense underfur and a fine oil on the surface. She sat up and looked around at the changed landscape, feeling perhaps a momentary sense of panic, since it seemed like another world. Not only were familiar things changed, but the snow muffled sounds and made the smells of the earth and scents of other animals fainter.

She watched a snowflake float down and land on the end of her warm nose and suddenly disappear. She snapped at the next one, and the next, and then she leaped at one, determined to catch it. But each snowflake melted into nothing in her mouth. She dived into the snow, snapping up mouthfuls, excitedly rolling and twisting at the same time. She decided that snow was good to eat, and it quenched her thirst. She had been thirsty for several days because the ponds and ditches had frozen over and ice was difficult to lick. Snow was a much more pleasant and easier way to satisfy her need for water.

The snow made hunting more difficult. The deeper it got, the harder it was for Vixie to travel, and for several days she would have to stay in a protective hollow or windbreak until the cold wind and sun had made a hard skin of more compact snow over which she could travel. She foraged constantly, picking up sick and starving birds, rabbits and mice. Occasionally she ran down unwary mice that came up to the surface of the snow. Their brown coats were easy to spot on the white blanket that covered the fields. Vixie also learned to listen and smell out mice in their snow burrows. Just like hunting them blind in long grass, she could rely on her keen hearing to locate them and then with one leap catch them under her forefeet.

The best places for food were around the farm, where the mice and rats multiplied even in the winter because they had plenty of food and warmth in the barn. Vixie sensed this, and the hungrier she became, the more daring she grew. By December she was paying regular visits to the farm and was on friendly terms with some of the cats, especially Ginger. The two farm dogs were always chained up and fast asleep in their kennels. They never saw Vixie on her early dawn hunting expeditions around the farm. Once her curiosity got the better of her, and she stole the remaining dinner scraps from the dogs' bowl and then left her "mark" in the bowl. Next morning the dogs were extremely excited when their sense of smell enabled them to piece things together. Ginger sat on the barn steps opposite and regarded them with curious indifference. Fortunately, the farmer didn't find Vixie's "mark" since one of the dogs, in its excitement, ate up the evidence!

Vixie continued to breakfast at the farm through the remaining winter, but she was always alert for danger, and anytime the dogs' chains rattled, she ran for cover. She never got used to this noise, although the clanging of the chains that restrained the milk cows didn't trouble her.

Vixie could climb the ladder to the hay loft easily. Early one morning she was nosing around in the loft, looking for mice and hens' eggs, when she heard a soft mewing noise. She had never heard anything like this before. She climbed on top of a bale of hay, and there from a small hollow in the hay, two yellow eyes stared out at her. The eyes suddenly grew bigger, and a hiss came from the darkness. She recognized the smell of Midnight, Ginger's beautiful mate. She had six little kittens. They must have been only a few days old, since their eyes weren't open. Midnight knew Vixie well, but she wasn't sure what the wild fox would do to her kittens. She might mistake them for fat mice and try to make a meal of them. But their tiny squeals and mews and sucking sounds filled Vixie with a tender curiosity. She lowered her ears, wagged her tail, and with a grin on her face, gave a panting, almost laughing, greeting as she rolled over onto her side. The cat understood some of this foxy language and stopped hissing. Vixie then squatted on her haunches and, with her inquisitive ears cocked to one side, watched Midnight tend her babies. Something in Vixie's mind told her the kittens were special little creatures, not to be eaten, but to be cleaned, kept warm, and fed. The sounds that kittens make are similar to the sounds made by baby foxes.

Vixie suddenly jumped up and left the loft, returning about half an hour later with a mouthful of mice for Midnight and her babies. Foxes bring food to their own babies, and the kittens had such a strong effect on Vixie that she was already moved to behave like a good mother-provider, although it would be some time before she had her own babies. Midnight purred and rolled over, allowing Vixie to sniff the kittens. She got very excited and started to dance and roll about the loft, making quite a noise. Suddenly one of the dogs began to bark, and quick as a flash, Vixie scurried down the ladder and out into the yard. The sun was up. She had stayed much longer than she should have. This was dangerous because the dogs were loose and the farmer and his hands were already at work around the yard. She clung to the shadows and disappeared in a red streak behind the barn. A breath later, she was speeding along the edge of the home meadow under cover of the thick hawthorn hedge, safe and still glowing from her encounter with Midnight and her babies.

One gray blustery March morning Vixie silently glided across the farmyard, heading for the barn and breakfast. She picked up a new smell in the cold air coming from a stable door, the top half of which had been blown open by the wind. She jumped up and hung on the edge of the half door with her chin and forepaws. Chickens! The farmer's wife had decided to raise some chickens so that she could make some extra money selling eggs to tourists and local people in the village. Vixie quivered all over, her senses tingling with the sight, smell and sound of the scrawny young birds. Without a further thought, she followed her instincts and leaped in among them. Instantly all the chickens began to run around, flapping their wings and clucking loudly. Vixie was completely confused by the ruckus she had caused. Whenever she tried to grab at one of the birds, another one seemed to get in her way or put her off. Birds acting up like this actually protect themselves by confusing and disorienting anyone trying to catch them.

But Vixie soon outsmarted them and decided to concentrate on one bird, a fat brown chick that was bigger, but slower, than the rest. Before she had a chance to grab it, that terrible light that she remembered so well from her night in the woods suddenly burned in her eyes.

The farmer was leaning over the half door, shotgun ready, and flashlight full on Vixie. She froze in one corner, and the chickens, also alarmed by the light, rushed to the same corner and huddled around her. The farmer couldn't shoot for fear he would kill all his wife's birds! The wily fox had outsmarted him again, he thought.

Vixie was petrified with fear. Not knowing what to do next, the farmer opened the stable door and, with his shotgun ready, ran at the chickens, hoping for a clear shot at Vixie. But the chickens—

Rhode Island reds—were a similar color to the fox. As they scattered in all directions, he became just as confused as Vixie was when she first jumped in among them.

Seizing her chance, Vixie raced between the farmer's legs, out the door, into the safe space of the dawning gray morning. Chickens and curses from the farmer spilled out into the yard. But he soon became quiet when he remembered that his wife had told him that a piece of old baler twine would not be enough to keep the upper door closed. He was lucky that the fox hadn't taken one of his wife's chickens, but from that day, he vowed that he would get even with all foxes.

It was a great pity that the farmer did not understand foxes and the other wild animals that lived on his land. In fact, he didn't really understand or care for his own domestic livestock. He saw them as a burden, and he saw wild animals as trespassers and enemies, especially foxes.

Vixie was so frightened that it would be a long time before she would go near the farm again. This would be no hardship now because spring was on the way and the meadows and hedgerows were coming alive again. There would be plenty to eat for everyone.

4
Spring Company

As Vixie made her way toward one of the many safe shelters in her range, she crossed a trail that was new and exciting, yet somehow familiar. Still pushed to keep running after her fearful experience at the farm, she didn't pause to investigate further until she crossed the trail again. This time the scent was strong and fresh. She was following the tracks of a large male red fox whose name, she would learn later, was Whitepaws. He was an unusual fox because his two hind feet were white, just as though he had sat in a pail of milk. They made him look very dashing indeed, setting off the white of his chin and tail tip. He was a wise, as well as handsome, fox and had returned to his favorite territory after spending the third winter of his life roaming far over the hills above the meadows.

Vixie didn't meet up with her new neighbor until early that evening. She was resting under a hedge and watching the stars come out one by one when the evening peace was abruptly shattered by a loud, tinny-sounding bark. This was followed by a series of shorter barks that sounded almost like a machine gun. The sounds carried for miles, and the farm dogs all around began barking. Vixie thought she heard another tinny bark farther along the valley, and then another, not so metallic this time, but instead ending in a coo-coo scream. Although Vixie did not recognize the call, it was her mother, and she seemed to be heading in Vixie's direction.

While her head was turned toward this new sound, she didn't notice something stalking silently toward her. Whitepaws took her by surprise, and Vixie reared backward, standing up on her hind legs and gaping with her mouth wide open in fear and threat. She clicked and hissed and coughed at the newcomer. Whitepaws backed off, lowered himself in a friendly way, and grinned. Vixie shyly turned away, frisking her tail to one side, and Whitepaws leaped toward her. She squirmed on the ground, waving her tail to and fro, and her excited panting turned into little screams and whines. She wriggled forward and kissed him on one side of the face. Whitepaws remained quite still and let her sniff him all over. He followed suit, after kissing her, and then he gently nibbled her eyelids and ears. A moment later he was gone into the night, in search of an older female fox whom he might court and mate with that springtime.

This was the first fox that Vixie had met in months, and her excitement at the encounter soon gave way to that old feeling of emptiness. But her stomach was empty too, so she forgot her loneliness and went looking for food. Her hunting expedition that night was unsuccessful. Perhaps the other animals were more wary after hearing foxes barking and calling to each other through the night. They continued their night and dawn calling for several days.

Each spring the male, or dog, foxes would return to their favorite places. They would let their presence be known by barking and establish their territories by marking them with their droppings, or "scats," and urine. This told other dog foxes to keep away because this land was already occupied. A dog fox would not tolerate another male in his territory. There isn't enough food in one territory to support more than one male and his family.

Their actions also attracted the female foxes, or vixens. Females don't roam far during the winter, and some of them even had dens cleaned out already; others had enlarged a rabbit burrow just in case they did mate and had a litter of cubs. This urge to prepare a den started first in the older foxes who had mated before. Vixie would not feel this urge for another three to four weeks.

Vixie wondered if she would see Whitepaws again. He was a courteous fox and might even be very affectionate if she got to know him better. As it was, Whitepaws found that another dog fox had beaten him and already established his territory in a place a little farther up the valley where

45

Whitepaws had hoped to find a mate. This rival fox was already courting Vixie's mother, and their screams and coos filled the twilight hours. Whitepaws took off into the hills again in search of food. Perhaps he would return to the meadows again soon.

A couple of days after her brief encounter with Whitepaws, Vixie was digging after some grubs and beetles under a rotten log. Just above her two jays were busy building their nest. The jays were disturbed by Vixie, and they started to make their raucous alarm call. Soon other birds—blackbirds, thrushes and an old magpie—joined them, and then all the birds started to swoop down upon Vixie. She had seen the birds do this once to Barnie, the owl, one morning when he was napping in a tall elm tree. The birds would also mob weasels and Ginger, the farm cat, in this way, their actions effectively driving off would-be bird or egg poachers.

Vixie took to her heels, since the birds were so persistent. They continued to mob her until she was halfway across the meadow, and then, one by one, they flew away. Such indignity for Vixie, to be chased by a flock of little birds, and she had meant them no harm, *that day* at least. No fox,

though, or weasel for that matter, would turn down the opportunity to eat a nestful of eggs or chicks. Hawks and owls will sometimes chase and catch adult birds, too, and this banding together by birds to attack a potential enemy is an inborn and very effective response.

Vixie took a nap in the middle of the meadow, out of sight, in a dry gully that smelled of mice and rabbits. But she didn't nap for long. That morning she had another surprise. The farmer had let the cows out for the first time after their long confinement in the barn through the winter. The cows were cavorting all over the meadow like young calves. Vixie watched these large, clumsy creatures in amazement, but when they came too close for comfort, she raced along the gully and into the next fallow field to resume her nap where it was quiet. Spring was a busy and exciting time.

About two weeks later Vixie was sniffing around a sandy mound of earth in a thick second growth of ash and willows. The mound was full of rabbit burrows, but as far as she could tell, no one lived there. Suddenly she began to dig, first with her forepaws, later with her nose and hind legs. She pushed the earth out and, with her jaws, tugged and tore at roots and buried rocks. The more she dug, the harder she dug, and soon she had enlarged one of the rabbit holes so that she could easily crawl in and turn around inside. She worked hard for a long time, and as though not satisfied with just one hole, she went a little way farther along the mound and enlarged another burrow.

Vixie was preparing dens. Pehaps she would have babies that springtime after all. Foxes will often enlarge a rabbit burrow or clean out an old fox den, or "earth," and prepare two or more so that they can move their house if the cubs get too flea-ridden. Also if they are disturbed by people, they will shift to another den. Many generations of foxes will use the same traditional dens each year, excavating a little more and making the passages longer and more complex over hundreds of years.

One day she heard Whitepaws barking, far off in the hills. Something inside Vixie seemed to burst and fill her with a new fire and eager confidence. The next time Whitepaws barked, she answered him, calling in the direction of his cry so that he could find her. He replied immediately, and Vixie gave a coo-coo scream and then nervously began to dig into the earth and rub her chin and chest in the fresh soil. The foxes con-

tinued to call to each other for some time, and
then Whitepaws was silent. Had he lost interest,
or had he, in his eagerness, fallen into a snare
along his trail?

Just before dawn, however, Vixie's fears were
dispelled. Whitepaws had kept silent as he got
closer to Vixie because he knew that the farmer
on whose land she lived would be out with gun

and traps if he heard the foxes calling to each other on his land. Vixie was alerted by a sudden rustling in the willow bushes, and Whitepaws appeared in full view. Vixie greeted him, and he responded with much more ardor than earlier. They then chased and gamboled through the bushes and up and over and around the mound many times. This was their courtship play, and it went off and on for several days, for at first Vixie was too shy and afraid even to let Whitepaws touch her. Soon, though, they were lying side by side in the sunlight on top of the mound, taking turns grooming and licking each other's faces and ears. Whitepaws kept inspecting the two dens, well hidden under thick bramble bushes. He seemed to approve of them, since he didn't dig around inside them at all. But he seemed anxious about them, knowing that there would soon be much work, and possibly many hungry mouths to feed.

5
Togetherness

Vixie and Whitepaws hunted together every morning and evening. They never really cooperated with each other like wolves and coyotes do, but sometimes Whitepaws would scare some field mice in front or to one side of him. Vixie would then move in to catch them. It looked as though Whitepaws were purposely "flushing" or driving the mice out so that Vixie could catch them. In fact, they were not really cooperating but, instead, simply sharing some advantages in being together, one getting the mice moving and the other pouncing on them. Often, though, they worked some distance apart, since mice and voles were still few and far between. Foxes have been known to follow behind a tractor, snapping up grubs and insects churned up by the plow. Like Vixie and Whitepaws' hunting the same field, this is taking advantage of a situation, rather than cooperation.

One day Whitepaws taught Vixie something new. Some wild mallard ducks had settled down to rest and dabble in a pond at the edge of the foxes' range. Whitepaws had seen them fly over and land on the pond earlier that day. He led Vixie stealthily toward the pond, then abruptly, about twenty leaps away from it, he stood up in full view of the ducks. The ducks saw him at once and became a little restless, but he was just far enough away so they were not scared off. Having caught their attention, the wily fox started jumping up in the air, diving and rolling on the ground, and even chasing his tail. Now and again he would completely disappear from the ducks' view, and then jump up like a jack-in-the-box. They were fascinated by his antics. Whitepaws seemed to act like a magnet, because the ducks swam to the edge of the pond to get a better look. Had Vixie known what he was doing, she might have crawled on her belly to the pond and grabbed one of the distracted ducks. As it was, with each leap and wriggle, Whitepaws was edging closer and closer to the unsuspecting ducks. They were so curious and seemed to be entertained by his "tolling" dance. Whitepaws could also "toll" rabbits, his actions somehow not releasing the flight instinct and enabling him to get close enough to suddenly leap on and capture his prey. Just at the right moment, and exactly at the right distance, he shot into the air and grabbed one of the ducks before the others flew off, quacking indignantly. Vixie was impressed and enjoyed the leftovers from Whitepaws' feast. Being a fox, he wouldn't share his food with anyone. But they both had a wild time chasing each other and rolling in the feathers afterward.

By going hunting with Whitepaws, Vixie also learned where to find birds' nests and fat beetles and grubs where the cows had been in the grass.

On their way home, Vixie paused now and again

to rest. She kept getting out of breath. Every time she stopped, she felt things moving in her stomach. She had experienced these wriggling sensations before, but they were much stronger and more persistent now. Whitepaws came over and sniffed her, and gave Vixie a gentle push with his nose. Soon they were back home in the sandy mound under the ash and willow trees. Vixie went straight into one of the dens, inspected it, and then went into the other, which she seemed to prefer, because she didn't come out all night.

Whitepaws stayed around the entrance to the den, or earth, and after his low "coo-coo" call didn't bring her out, he went off hunting alone. When he returned, he had a mouthful of mice for his mate, and although she could smell them at the entrance, Vixie wouldn't come out. So Whitepaws buried the mice under a clump of willows. They would make a nice snack later.

In the warm darkness of the earth, Vixie was going through the first stages of labor. Her entire system, prepared for the birth of young, was taking over, and Vixie lay on one side, panting and straining occasionally. The straining and pushing became more frequent and intense, and between each bout Vixie would lick herself and occasionally push the earth down with her nose. Then, suddenly, her whole body tensed and something burst between her legs. She licked furiously. It was the water bag in which a cub is born. Moments later, something dark and steaming warm was squirming on the earth floor of the den.

As she licked the small baby dry, it began to breathe and then cry and cough, giving little bubbly sounds as its lungs were cleared of fluids. Her licking seemed to stimulate the cub, and it breathed and cried more vigorously than ever. Vixie cut the umbilical cord which had joined the baby to its mother and freed the drying cub from its birth envelope of membranes and placenta. These she carefully ate and then gave her attention again to the baby.

As Vixie licked the face of the cub, it was drawn by its mother's warmth and began to root into the fur of her flanks. Still too young to hear or see, the newborn cub knew enough to crawl toward the warmth of its mother's side, and once there, its sensitive nose and lips found a teat. It held on and, with increasing strength and certainty, began to suck, at first noisily. But later it had a sure hold, and as the first milk began to come more freely, its whole body seemed to fill and tense with the energy flowing from Vixie in her rich milk. For the cub, finding its mother's teat meant survival.

Gently, Vixie licked her first cub between its legs. This made it strain and eventually pass a little water. She cleaned up the mess and swallowed so that the baby wouldn't soil the den. It would pass something only when its mother licked it, and in this way the den and cubs would be kept clean.

After another half hour, Vixie began to strain and push again, and the wonderful birth cycle was repeated. This time, before she had the second cub dry, two more were born in rapid succession, and she was kept busy cleaning and drying them. By noon the whole process was over, and Vixie was able to rest with her four new cubs alternately sucking and sleeping at her side.

Outside, unaware of the great event beneath the earth, the birds were still singing and newly emerged butterflies were trying out their bright wings in the gentle spring breeze. Whitepaws was lying against a tree root close to the den, listening to a burrowing mole's progress a few inches under the grass. Not once did he take his eyes away from the den entrance. Growing impatient and curious, he went to the hole and called to Vixie. She

crawled out and greeted him in a tired, sleepy
way. He sniffed her all over and learned that she
had given birth, but his nose couldn't tell him how
many cubs there were. She gaped her mouth open
in mild threat, and she pushed him away when
he made to go down into the den. Vixie was feeling protective toward her babies. She wouldn't
allow Whitepaws to visit them for several days.
So he groomed her face for a few minutes, and
then she went back to tend to the litter.

Whitepaws, knowing his responsibilities, went off to hunt that evening and came back with many mice and voles. Vixie made short work of them. She already felt the drain of energy in producing milk for the hungry cubs. Whitepaws ate from the store of mice he had caught and hidden earlier that day. Quite often, male foxes will leave their mates before the cubs are born and never share the burden of parenthood. Why some males stay and others do not remains a mystery. Are some couples more devoted than others? Or is it only when there is an abundance of food so that it is easy for the mother to provide for the cubs that the male's help is unnecessary?

Night and day, for the next few days, Whitepaws worked hard providing food for his hungry family. At about the time the cubs' eyes opened, around eight days of age, Vixie went off hunting alone one morning. Whitepaws stayed behind to baby-sit. Before she left, Vixie called her mate to the den and allowed him to visit his children for the first time. He was very excited, his nose and ears tingling in the den as the sweet-hay smelling cubs mewed and nuzzled against his lowered head. After thoroughly sniffing, licking and cleaning each pup, even though they were already clean from Vixie's care, he crawled out of the den and lay on top of the mound, keeping a lookout for danger.

From that day on, the two foxes would take turns baby-sitting and hunting. The cubs were never left alone. During the day, and especially around feeding time, the entrance to the den echoed more and more with the growls and clicks and screams of the cubs. They were growing fast and now had needle-sharp teeth that made nursing an uncomfortable and brief affair for Vixie. The cubs squabbled in the darkness for pieces of food that Vixie or Whitepaws brought in for them. Both mother and father threw up partly digested food for the babies, and gradually, they would be weaned this way. As they grew older and stronger, they would be given whole mice to eat, and sometimes even live mice to practice stalking.

6

Family Life

Early one morning, when the cubs were about three weeks old, Whitepaws went into the den and regurgitated some food for them. He left quickly because all four little spitfires started fighting. Like fragments from an explosion in the earth, the cubs came into the open for the first time. One by one, they spilled out into the gentle dawn light. The last to leave was Wylie, the greediest and biggest of the four. He stayed behind to finish the meal that he had successfully kept from his brother and two sisters.

Each cub blinked in the rush of pale morning light, and the sudden impact of so many intense sounds and smells, of which they were only vaguely aware in the den, made them cower and crawl on their bellies toward Whitepaws and Vixie, who were sitting a leap away from the entrance. They soon adjusted to the new world, and the higher the sun climbed into the sky, the more they explored the exciting sounds, smells and sights around the den. Although they wobbled and often fell over as they crawled and sometimes tried to run and jump, with each step their movements became smoother and faster. With each step they learned something new. They had much to experience, for in a few months they would have to fend for themselves.

All the cubs were outgoing and showed little fear. Aesop, Wylie's brother, caught a beetle that first day. He was a quick, intelligent fox, while Wylie, although just as bright, tended to forget himself and get into trouble. He kept wandering off too far from the den, and Whitepaws or Vixie would have to carry him back when he got lost and started to coo-coo cry. The girl cubs, Tippy and Melany, were just as quick and inquisitive, but were less aggressive than the boys and always stayed closer to the den. Melany was a dark-colored fox; instead of being red, her coat was a beautiful dark brown-black. She would grow up to be a silver fox. She was the most docile of the four cubs and also the most generous and playful. Her sister, Tippy, had a straw-blond coat, and the white tip on the end of her tail was much bigger than on the others. Tippy seemed to be aware of this and would spend hours chasing and catching her tail.

The cubs spent more and more of their waking hours playing and exploring outside the den. They chased, stalked, ambushed and wrestled with each other, sometimes chasing imaginary mice, other times real mice, in the grass. Their games often ended in squabbles, especially when more than two were playing together. Consequently, Wylie spent most of his time playing with Aesop, and Melany with Tippy. The boys were bigger and rougher anyway.

One of their favorite games was to stalk White-paws' tail when he was sunning himself. The white tip on the end of his thick, bushy tail was a super target for the cubs to attack. Whitepaws, with the cubs in the corner of his eye, would lie very still and just twitch the tip of his tail for them. They seemed to be much rougher with Vixie's tail, and

as soon as they started to pull hard on it, she would either run off a short way or lie on top of her tail so they couldn't get at it.

In late May, when the cubs were about four weeks old, Vixie moved them to the other den at

the far end of the mound. Whitepaws followed, pushing stragglers with his nose and carrying some of their playthings in his mouth—a rabbit's paw, a shred of tractor tire, and a half-eaten shoe that Vixie had found under a hedge. The old den was getting smelly and full of fleas, and the cubs soon settled down in clean comfort.

They were exploring around their new home when Whitepaws gave a low bark-whistle. This warning signal meant danger to the cubs. Immediately they ran and hid in the den while the two adults found hiding places in the willows. It was the farmer, with one of his dogs. He was searching around the mound, looking for a den, and he chuckled to himself when he found the den that the foxes had only just abandoned. There were fresh signs around, and he thought the foxes were still using it. He listened at the entrance, but heard nothing. Just to be sure, he fired his shotgun into the hole to kill whatever might be inside. Then he threw some meat on the ground, meat covered with strychnine that would kill any fox that ate the poisoned bait.

Fortunately, he had found only the old den and the cubs were still safe. But his dog, clearly more aware than its master, picked up the foxes' trail leading to the new den. The dog started to lead the farmer toward the foxes, when out of the willows raced Whitepaws, aiming a volley of sharp barks at dog and master. The dog fox exposed himself completely to the hunters and took off leisurely across the meadow with his tail high, hoping to lure them away from the den.

The farmer cursed his empty gun. Quickly reloading it, he ran out of the bushes and chased after Whitepaws. Meanwhile, his dog started to eat the poison bait! The farmer soon lost Whitepaws, and when his dog caught up with him, it was already drooling at the mouth and staggering. The foxes had outsmarted him again and poisoned his dog, he thought! In a blind fury, the farmer fired his gun at the blue sky and rushed back to the farm with the dog under his arm.

Frantically, he telephoned the local veterinarian for help, and by good fortune he was at a neighboring farm treating a sick cow. Within minutes, he arrived and gave the dog an antidote for the poison. He was just in time to save the dog's life because strychnine is a very quick-acting poison.

The animal doctor then gave the farmer a long lecture about the cruel use of poisons like strychnine and asked him why he wanted to kill the foxes on his land. He also pointed out that other animals—birds, weasels, cats and dogs—could eat the bait and be poisoned, too. The farmer just shrugged and, scowling, said that he could do anything he liked on his land because it was his property.

The fox family was lucky not to have been troubled more by their fox-hating landlord that spring, but he had been busy "improving" his farm so that he would have even less work to do. His spring project was to tear up all the hedges and trees, field by field, with his tractor and put up barbed-wire fencing instead. Being a lazy farmer, he couldn't be bothered trimming and tying up the hedgerows that enclosed his fields. He had seen pictures of the large cornfields of the Midwest that stretched for miles without a tree or hedgerow in sight, just barbed wire, corn, and little else. But the ignorant farmer didn't know that he was destroying the homes of thousands of insects and birds—and at the same time making it harder for the foxes and weasels to find food. Removing all the trees and hedges would disturb the delicate balance of nature. With nowhere to build their nests, the birds would leave. Since many of these birds ate certain insects and seeds from the fields and kept their numbers controlled, these insects and plants might become too abundant in their absence. Other insects and plants might be crowded out, and in a few years there might not be the right vegetation around for the rabbits and mice to eat. They might starve and so, in turn, would the weasels and foxes. Unknowingly then, the farmer was going to destroy a complex food chain and cause unnecessary hardship to countless animals. The birds and insects would either die or find another home somewhere else, and the foxes and weasels, too, would be forced to move out. But where could all the animals go, since all available living space in the surrounding countryside was already occupied?

Before he had stripped out two small fields and put up wire fencing, he was forced to abandon his project. Because he cared so little for his cattle and they were in such poor condition, a severe epidemic started in his spring calves and spread rapidly into his main dairy herd. Many of them died and others stopped producing milk. They were his only source of income. This was the last straw for him and an excuse to sell out. The farm was auctioned, and he and his wife went to make a new life in the city.

But what would the new owner be like? Would he be a more efficient fox hunter and a "modern" farmer who liked to have no trees on his barbed-wire-fenced pastures?

7
Growing Up

The foxes knew nothing of these things that indirectly were to have such an influence on their lives and future. They continued to prosper, the cubs growing perceptibly each day, and each day bringing them new and exciting experiences.

Learning is survival for all wild animals, and infancy is a fine time for school, as well as play.

Wylie learned not to snap at black-and-yellow-striped flies that buzzed, or else he would get stung! Tippy discovered how to catch grasshoppers in midflight. She was as agile as a cat, while her littermates could only pounce and hope to snap one before it took off. All the cubs learned not to bite each other too hard, because by eight weeks of age they could kill each other with their long, sharp teeth. They learned all the calls and silent body language of foxes, and they learned what all the noises and smells meant in their green, happy world.

Small things that moved usually meant something to eat, and the young foxes responded instinctively by chasing, leaping and grabbing. But not all small things were supposed to be eaten, and the cubs had to learn this through trial and error. No amount of pawing and pushing would get a box turtle to open up, even though Wylie spent nearly a full day trying, long after the others had given up.

They all enjoyed eating frogs and soon recognized them by the way they hopped. One day something hopped in front of Melany, and confident that it was a frog, she grabbed it. Her mouth erupted with the most bitter and sickening taste she had ever experienced. It was a toad, which, unlike a frog, has a chemical defense that will repel most predators. Some toads are even poisonous. The other cubs ran over and investigated, and each tasted the toad. They would never bother toads again. Such experiences not only helped them learn what was good to eat and what was dangerous or unpleasant to attack, but also helped them save their energy.

They would not, for example, chase a large buck rabbit from halfway across the field. They would work slowly and stealthily, using cover to hide themselves. Nor would they go out hunting for one prey alone and nothing else (like most human hunters do) They learned to be ready for anything: a baby bird that had fallen out of a nest; a fat grasshopper sunning himself; a bush full of sunburst black raspberries; a mouse in the grass; a dead pheasant in a ditch. They became as versatile in finding all manner of foods as was the variety of the things they could eat. Nothing is wasted in nature, and the fox cubs, through instinct and learning, soon became a part of the complex chain of life in the quiet summer pastures of rural Pennsylvania.

The cubs continued to learn about all the things

around them that made up their world. They learned to recognize the alarm calls of birds, like the blackbird, which could mean that a hunter was near. The silence of the birds and of the mice in the grass could also mean danger. They learned how to dig under sun-dried cow droppings and collect insects and grubs that feasted there. They also learned to hide surplus food and favorite play items and, more important still, to remember where they had buried them. Using all their senses—sight, hearing, taste, smell, and even touch (with a paw or a nose)—they quickly learned what they would need to survive the winter and grow into healthy adults.

By June they were no longer living in a den. Instead they used a small clearing on top of the mound, where they would play and rest and wait for their parents to bring them food.

Early one Sunday morning in early September, the cubs were alerted to a sound they had never heard before. It was the hu-hu-hu of a hunting horn. Vixie and Whitepaws, who had just brought them a meal, immediately tensed and gave their alarm call. For a while the horn sound seemed to circle them, but the circle was getting smaller and smaller around the foxes. Vixie took off in one direction and Whitepaws in the opposite direction. The cubs understood the message: Split up and run for your life.

Soon after, their mound in the willows was plundered by a pack of panting, drooling foxhounds. The lead dogs circled where the cubs had been lying, confused as to what direction to take. Whitepaws had apparently run in a great circle as though on purpose so the dogs would perhaps choose to follow his trail. Being a dog fox, his scent was much stronger than Vixie's or any of the cubs. But because the cubs were so frightened, they were also leaving a strong scent.

Since the foxes' trails went in all directions, most of the dogs took after Whitepaws. Three of the hounds followed Wylie's scent. They caught up with him crossing one corner of a field, and he dived into a bramble bush. There, he keeled over and played dead. Young foxes "play possum" like this when they are really scared. The three dogs eagerly circled the bramble bush and tried to break in, but the thorns and twisted branches kept them out. Brutus, the lead dog, began to make some headway, and when he saw Wylie playing dead, he started to tear and pull at the brambles, feeling no pain in his frenzied excitement.

Suddenly, no more than fifty leaps away, Whitepaws came running past, tail high in the air, with the rest of the hounds baying half a field away and in hot pursuit. He seemed to be enjoying it, like going for a Sunday jog. Seeing their companions close to the fox, the three dogs joined the pack and forgot all about Wylie.

The other three cubs were in safe hiding, but Vixie was still running. She, too, started to run instinctively in a great circle, her path cutting across the line that Whitepaws was taking. As soon as he picked up her scent, he ran a little way along her trail, which passed close to a stone wall by the farm. Then he backtracked, jumped on top of the wall and ran along a little way. The hounds, still half a field away, didn't see this clever maneuver.

When they reached the point where Vixie and Whitepaws' scent trails crossed, there was total confusion. The hounds started to mill around, not knowing which trail to take. Some wanted to go after Vixie, others, after Whitepaws, but White-paws just seemed to vanish. Several people on heaving horses arrived on the scene, adding to the confusion.

The master of hounds, a red-faced man with whiskers, snapped encouraging commands to his dogs, and his assistant, called the whipper-in, cracked his whip over the dogs to encourage them even more. Two of the dogs then decided to head for home, and another pair sneaked off to the barn for a rest. The other huntsmen grew impatient, and each started giving suggestions as to where the fox might have gone.

Two excited children on fat ponies caught up with the rest of the hunt, eager to see the hounds get a fox. This was their first hunt, and if by a slim chance a fox was caught, they would be given a special prize treat that would make good telling at school. Their faces would be painted with fresh fox blood, and each would be given a paw as a souvenir! Surely, if either of them had really known Vixie, they would have been sickened by the thought of this old and gory custom.

At least this Sunday was a good one for the foxes. For Whitepaws it was simple to outwit fifteen dogs and twelve riders and horses, especially with Vixie to help him. It was an amusing, but sobering, sight to see so many domestic animals and people outwitted by a small fox.

Brutus, the lead hound, eventually discovered Whitepaws' ruse and jumped up on the wall and, like a drunken rider, followed the fox's trail. The other hounds followed, somehow making progress

along the wall even though they fell off it more times than they were on it. The trail went from the wall right into the farmyard, up into the loft, into the milking parlor, and then back to the wall where it had started. Again the hounds were confused. Whitepaws had doubled back along the wall and had jumped up into an oak tree, and had a ringside view of the chaos in the farmyard!

The new farmer was out for the day. His wife came out in a pink rage, since she had just cleaned out the milking parlor. What she said to the huntsmen did not befit such a beautiful Sabbath morning, although it was certainly appropriate for them and their "sport." So the hunt was called off, and the foxes were left in peace again for a while.

That night the foxes called to each other and soon met together at a familiar spot, under the old oak tree where Vixie was born. They all slept, each one reliving the experiences of the day in dreams that made legs, tails and ears twitch and jerk as though the hounds were still after them. None of the foxes knew what great changes were to take place. Changes that would affect their lives and the lives of their children.

8

Peace and Continuity

All four cubs were playing hide-and-seek one full-moon evening around a thicket of young silver birch trees. Each fox took turns leaping onto the trunk of a long-dead and fallen oak tree, then jumping down, often right on top of a companion, and, finally, racing through the birch trees and back to begin the game again.

Melany was distracted by a beetle clicking somewhere inside the rotting log, and she started to nose and paw after it. She did not see Wylie readying himself to pounce on her until the last minute, and by then it was too late. She had the beetle in her mouth and it was hers! Until she had finished with it, she wouldn't want to play anymore. Wylie, of course, didn't know this and received a hard nip from Melany, who dropped and lost her beetle. Both annoyed, the two cubs started to scream and squabble, and they did not see Aesop and Tippy suddenly dive for cover. Nor did they hear the grunting, scraping sounds coming from under the roots of the fallen oak.

A broad, flat squint-eyed face emerged, steaming and wheezing monstrously in the twilight. After the head came a long, low, broad body on short, powerful legs. It seemed to squeeze out of the earth like brown toothpaste and then pause, lifting its head from side to side, sniffing the air. This was Wheezer, the old sow badger, and she was as powerful as she looked, and worse still, she was annoyed by the rumpus that Wylie and Melany were making.

Aesop gave a low bark whistle warning, but the

two squabbling foxes were so wrapped up in what they were doing that they did not hear. Then they saw the broad, striped face and beady eyes of Wheezer coming right at them over the edge of the log. The old badger meant them no harm. She was curious and just wanted a little peace around her den site. Seeing Wheezer right in front of them, Wylie and Melany leaped straight up into the air and somersaulted over the astonished head of Wheezer and dashed back through the birch trees to their own den.

Aesop and Tippy, in true fox style, were still stuck by their insatiable curiosity to their hiding place. They watched Wheezer sniff carefully all over the log where they had been playing. Wheezer seemed to cough and splutter, and this brought on a flurry of scraping and grunting noises from beneath the upturned roots of the tree, and four baby badgers came rolling out. One by one they scrambled onto the log and started up a whole series of complex games: King of the Castle, where one would try to push another off; a kind of leap-frog, where one would roll over the other; and then one by one, starting at the higher end of the log, they took turns sliding down it.

Aesop and Tippy were not able to look much

longer because the wind changed, blowing their scent toward the sensitive nostrils of old mother Wheezer. As soon as she caught wind of them, she trundled toward them, her apparent clumsiness making it seem as though she were going quite slowly. But she was deceptively swift and agile. The foxes took to their heels, hearing Wheezer crashing through the trees behind, but she was no match for their speed. The cubs realized that badgers like to keep to themselves, and from that night on they kept away from Wheezer's place.

The next morning the cubs had another surprise. They met their first skunk, and it would be the last that they would ever try to play with. Whitepaws and Vixie had left them under a hedgerow for the morning, and the busy cubs were poking around for things to eat and play with, when along the hedgerow, in broad daylight for all to see and without a care in the world, waltzed Simon skunk. Now Simon, with his black-and-white warning colors (which meant: Look out, I can harm you!), was quite confident that the cubs would take heed and keep away. But he didn't know that they didn't know, except Wylie. His experience with black-and-yellow stinging insects made him think that black and white might be a

83

warning of danger, too. So he held back while the other three, quivering with excitement, edged forward and began to circle around Simon.

Taken aback, Simon froze and stuck his tail up as a warning threat, pointing his behind at Tippy.

She thought it would be fun to try and grab his tail, and since Simon seemed to be inviting this, she lunged at his arched tail. But it was like jumping into a brick wall. Simon shot a full load of his scent into her face, and her nose, mouth and

eyes and mind were lost in the sweet, overpowering and stinging spray. Shocked and helpless, Tippy tried frantically to wipe the scent off her face with her paws. Then she rolled in the grass, which only helped to rub in and spread the stink over her body.

The other cubs were rooted to the spot. They had never seen or smelled anything like this before and were spellbound by Tippy's hysterical behavior. Meanwhile, Simon collected his cool and, with great dignity, walked slowly and confidently away. He had taught the foxes to respect his kind—at a distance, that is—and the smell that Tippy would carry around would be a constant reminder for the cubs for several days to come!

About a week after the incident with the horse and hound people, a change occurred in the family life of the foxes. It was fall, which meant breakup time. Whitepaws went off to hunt alone one morning and never returned. He was off to his wide-open range in the hills again, where he would spend another winter. Vixie paid one more visit to the cubs and left them with a small token of food. The cubs sensed that it was time to make it alone, and one by one, they left to find their fortunes elsewhere.

Tippy and Aesop took off down the valley, while Wylie and Melany stayed around for a couple of days before they, too, went their separate ways. Each left with a wealth of experience gained from their time together in the instructive safety and affection of Vixie and Whitepaws. But the ties of affection were not strong enough to keep them together. Their life-style is adapted to living much of the year alone, especially through the winter, when there is so little food that each must scavenge for himself.

Vixie must have felt the loss of Whitepaws and her children, but it was a relief not to have four hungry mouths to feed. Soon the cold weather would come, and she would have to work hard again in order to survive the winter. She wondered about the farm. Would she dare go back and hunt mice in the barn again after the terrible scare with the chickens? Vixie decided to snoop around her old haunts the next morning, and she was surprised by a whole new set of smells and sights. There were two new cats, in addition to Ginger and Midnight. The previous farmer had apparently drowned all of Midnight's kittens. His two dogs had gone, and in their kennel lay a large, unchained collie dog who actually wagged his tail at Vixie. She skittered away, being unsure of dogs after her experience with the hounds.

The new owner was a farmer in the real sense of the word. He had moved in only a short while ago, but already he had whitewashed and cleaned everything, had some of the uprooted hedges replanted, and had put up a big sign which read: NO HUNTING OR POACHING: TRESPASSERS WILL BE PROSECUTED. Vixie, of course, couldn't read, but her new landlord knew the value of foxes, weasels, rabbits and birds. He had removed all the rusted and broken farm equipment, old tractors and cars that cluttered half a meadow and was going to plow this and plant all kinds of organically grown vegetables next spring.

This farmer wouldn't use any insecticides on his plants. He knew that many of these, like DDT, could kill birds and mice and certain insects who kept other destructive insects off his plants. A few insect marks on an apple or a piece of corn wouldn't matter to him. You find a worm only in a good apple! He also knew that if he let part of the grazing land rest and renourish itself naturally it would do better than if he poured tons of artificial fertilizers on it.

This farmer wanted to live with nature, and he knew that his land would do better if he let the wild animals on it live in harmony with his own domestic livestock.

He also knew that foxes could transmit rabies and perhaps carry foot-and-mouth disease, both deadly diseases. There would always be diseases and the risk of infection, but sensible care and feeding and vaccinations of animals could greatly reduce the risk. He saw no point in destroying wild animals to prevent diseases. The benefits they provided far outweighed the possibility that they might carry a disease. Worst for the foxes was distemper and hepatitis, which they could easily get from unvaccinated farm dogs, and Vixie was lucky not to have picked something up the time she boldly stole the remains of the dogs' dinner that gray winter morning a year ago.

Vixie briefly surveyed the farm, enjoying the new smells and feeling more relaxed, perhaps because the domestic animals there seemed more content with their lot. As she departed into the growing silver light of morning, she jumped onto the wall under the tree where Whitepaws had

eluded the hunt. She looked out across the meadows, her sleek wild form silhouetted against the sky. She faced her world, not a wilderness, but a tamed place, domesticated over hundreds of years by man the farmer. She was a link with the past, with a wilderness now gone. She and her kind had held on to life and adapted to man and all the many changes that he had made to the natural world. For a time, perhaps, things would stay the same, and at least one farmer recognized and respected Vixie for what she was.

The first birds of morning were beginning to sing. Vixie raised her head and barked three times at the pale moon, then faded into the will-o'-the-wisp mist over the grass. The farmer heard her in his sleep, and his dreams filled with a new hope that perhaps his children, too, would know the beauty of nature, of the wild animals that still remained in the green cage world that man controlled. A green world for which he cared and understood more than most.

About the Author

Dr. Michael Fox has personally raised red, gray, and arctic foxes, as well as timber wolves, coyotes, and jackals, and he bases much of the information in *Vixie* on first-hand observations. Dr. Fox is a noted authority on animal behavior, combining the background of a degree from London's Royal Veterinary School and a PhD in psychology from London University with a profound concern for the well-being and conservation of wildlife.

Dr. Fox is an associate professor of psychology at Washington University. He has written several books on animal behavior, including *The Wolf, Understanding Your Dog,* and *Behavior of Wolves, Dogs, & Related Canids.*

Dr. Fox, his wife, Bonnie, and two children, Wylie and Camilla, make their home in St. Louis, Missouri.

About the Artist

Free-lance artist Jennifer Perrott's illustrations have appeared in the New York *Times*. Many of her illustrations for *Vixie* are based on actual photographs by Dr. Fox of foxes in motion.

Jennifer Perrott makes her home in Arlington, Virginia.

DATE DUE

GAYLORD   PRINTED IN U.S.A.